Charon

A Modern Myth

By DC Fidler

Published by DCFidler Publishing

2024

Published by DCFidler Publishing
300 West Fifth Street #647
Charlotte, NC 28202

DCFidlerpublishing@gmail.com

Printed in the United States of America
by Kindle Direct Publishing

10, 9, 8, 7, 6, 5, 4, 3, 2, 1

Cover art: *River Styx* engraving by Kevin D. Marlow
and Photo by Donald C. Fidler
from the Donald C. Fidler Collection

WGAW Registration: 2246097
Library of Congress Registration: 1-13565262661

ISBN: (paperback) 979-8-9864610-7-6
ISBN: (ebook) 979-8-9864610 -8-3

Appreciation

Thank you to my wonderful writing teachers: Doris Betts, Max Steele, Wallace Kaufman, and writers-in-residence James Dickey and Robert Anderson at the University of North Carolina at Chapel Hill. That was decades ago, but your caring presences continue to instruct me.

Thank you to Sandi Constantino-Thompson for your wonderful lessons about editing and your infectious enthusiasm that keeps me writing and rewriting long hours each day.

Thank you to RJ Casey, Andrew Trumbull, Ben Hogan, Paul Rashid, and Travis Teffner, my sometimes co-writers and writing consultants, who are consistently my audience when I write solo.

Thank you to my numerous restaurant and coffee-shop buddies who nourish me with food as well as nourish me with enthusiasm for writing.

Thank you to the Charlotte Writers Club for the many writing classes and critiques from club writers.

Thank you to my friend Seth Rollins for re-introducing me to Greek mythology.

Charon

A Modern Myth

Charon
A Modern Myth

By DC Fidler

1. A FAMILY DEATH

Thirty-five-year-old Judge Nicholas Charon's mother was dead. A morning's mobile voicemail stated such.

"Message for Nicholas Charon in Charlotte. This is Dr. Rami Fernando's office at Rush Medical Center in Chicago. I regret to inform you that your mother, Eleni Charon, died at 5:17 this morning."

No euphemisms of "passed" or "is no longer with us" or "has gone home to God" as might be offered by crafty, soft-spoken funeral-home directors. The pithy message clearly stated, "died." Undisputed death.

The voicemail concluded, "For more information, call 312-942-5000."

What more information could one need, Nicholas pondered. Eleni Charon was dead. His mother no longer existed. Was there a reason to learn what she was wearing or how her last breaths sounded?

"All rise," the Bailiff called out as Nicholas entered the county district courtroom, a room far from being the lofty venue he desired to rule.

Although Nicholas was usually adept at turning his back on life's wrinkles and sour childhood-memories, he struggled to rally from this morning's voicemail. His necktie was a noose, choking blood flow to his brain. He could not shut out his mother's voice from their last phone call. "You are the last hope for our family tree. Make me a grandmother."

Nicholas had hung up on her, thinking, Another gargantuan demand from a contrary woman that I have no intention of fulfilling. If she were here today and made the same demand, I would hang up on her again.

"Your Honor?" a voice in the courtroom hailed, fraily pulling Nicholas into the present.

Nicholas glared toward the direction of the voice and snorted. The attorney flinched. Judge Charon's reputation was one of enforcing court decorum and dealing out justice with barbarity in the manner second-rate actors portray mob bosses and dictators.

Providence plucked Nicholas's mind back to his mother's Greektown attic, rummaging through her Victorian travel trunk. Musty papers, frayed and unlabeled photos of unknown people, shreds of cloth, a handful of Greek coins, a Buffalo Bills' football trading card, a pair of rotting ballerina shoes about which he had no clue. A certificate that unveiled before his mother birthed him as a single, unwed mother, she changed her name from Eleni Anagnostopoulou to Eleni Charon. Easier to pronounce? Fewer letters for filling out government and corporate forms? Love for the Carl Charon on the water-stained football card? Charon? Coincidence? An imaginary romance? A forbidden romance?

"Your Honor?" the defendant's state-provided lawyer yelled, followed by guttural throat clearing, yanking the judge back into Charlotte's Mecklenburg County District Court. "Have you arrived at a decision about my client's sentence? Sir?"

Nicholas stared at the lawyer's unironed shirt, at the several days of scruff on the defendant's face, thinking, I deserve better than this. I earned sophisticated cases involving sophisticated people.

He gazed at the ceiling as if Elysium would provide an answer, but heard the heavy-smoker breathing of the cryptic matron who had touted he was of Greek ancestry and frightened him as a toddler with myths of severed heads and one-eyed giants.

"Your Honor?" the lawyer screamed loudly enough that a hallway guard poked his head through the door to assure a brouhaha had not broken out.

Nicholas's attention dawdled from ceiling to thumbing through a document. "Your client pleads guilty, correct?"

"He does, your Honor. He is throwing himself at the mercy of this court."

Nicholas listlessly waved a finger before the defendant as if conducting him in music or hypnotizing him. "Your third time before the court, am I correct?"

The man conjured up sad puppy eyes, hoping to wheedle Nicholas for mercy.

"Three times you purchased libations for women straddling bar stools. Each time, you became sickeningly intoxicated, grabbed the women's wrists, and towed them toward the door."

"They owed me," the handcuffed man muttered, retracting his head like a turtle to appear more pitiful.

"After they refused to leave with you, you threatened them."

"No sir. I showed 'em my stag-antler hunting knife. Onliest gift Grandpop ever give me."

"These signed affidavits state the entire pub felt threatened by your rage. You, feral fiend, owe civilization for feeding and attempting to educate you. Your debt mounted to no avail. Tenacious instruction is stringently required."

"Ten what?"

Nicholas slammed his gavel as if propelling a nail down

to the underworld. "Four thousand dollars. One year."

"One year," the man screamed and turned on his lawyer. "You swore if I pled guilty, I'd get probation."

"Officer, escort ..." Nicholas referred to the paper before him. "Escort Mr. Horvat back to his holding cell."

Horvat spat toward Nicholas. "You fucking, asshole. You'll burn in hell."

Mr. Horvat's screaming echoed for the minutes it took to drag him along the hallway.

"Mr. Linden?" Nicholas motioned for Horvat's lawyer to approach. "I know our public system grossly underpays you, but when you appear in my court, your shirt will be ironed, the top button fastened, your tie properly knotted, and you will not appear with droopy eyelids as if pulled from nursing a hangover while sleeping on a pile of alley trash."

"Yes sir," the lawyer mumbled, staring downward, hoping the judge could not see his shoes, both scuffed and one unlaced.

"Even five feet away, I smell you. Use deodorant for God's sake."

"Yes, your Honor."

"Next case."

Nicholas eyed the next lawyer and client. The lawyer was dressed in a decent jacket but wearing a bright-flowered beach shirt beneath. Not tucked in.

His client was draped in what once had been a white T-shirt, but now was coffee color with a rip and a spaghetti-sauce stain.

2. LAST CASE OF THE DAY

Before asserting judgment on the day's final case, Nicholas glanced at the faces of the seven people in his court. All women: the defendant—simply but properly outfitted—her pony-tailed lawyer fresh out of law school, the buzz-cut bailiff, an escorting guard, the court reporter, and two church-going-grandmotherly types sitting in the galley. Unusual to have all women in attendance, but not unfamiliar that all eyes glared his direction. Only the court reporter was not staring daggers. She was, however, grimacing as if stenography were as painful as appendicitis.

Nicholas felt he was treading water in a sea of disdain. What had he said? Done? Was it his reputation for handing out harsh judgments? "Cold-hearted," the *Charlotte Observer* had printed. "Ruthless," *WBTV News* had broadcast. There were stories of defendants and attorneys responding with profane outbursts—a sometimes truth woven into court gossip.

Nicholas peered over his reading glasses at the defendant and her lawyer. "Please stand."

He gauged the age of the lawyer. She resembled high-school students, young enough to be her client's daughter. "Your client pleads guilty, correct?'

"Correct, your Honor."

Nicholas aimed a knuckle at the defendant. "You claim you merely shoplifted candy bars and a pair of high-end running shoes—'borrowed' I believe was your word—to feed and clothe five children. A similar claim you professed in past brushes with the law. You, madam, should have refrained from having children. Planned ahead so that getting pregnant did not exceed your capabilities. But you either chose—God knows for what reason—to become pregnant or were careless beyond this court's comprehension."

Nicholas paused as the court's rear door opened, permitting cool air to rush in with the sound of a giant spirit exhaling pent-up air. All heads rotated and gaped at a demure, hunched, elderly woman draped in an overly-large, nun-style black cloak. As she hobbled to the rear bench, Nicholas assessed she was as short as a small child. Her smoker-yellowed hair accentuated her features: absent eyebrows and gray-blue pupils specked with white plaques. Surely, she is blind, Nicholas thought, and yet, she appears to be peering my direction—no. Not peering. Reaching for my soul.

He felt compelled to demand the invader reveal her identity, but disciplined himself that this case—like all lower court cases—is open to the public.

Nicholas took a deep breath and refocused upon the defendant. "Our community enacted with misplaced sympathies for you, no doubt a woman in a wretched situation, but one who exceeded this court's patience. You embraced a life of poor choices and must endure consequences. I trust social services, your family, a church, perhaps the state will step forth and assume custody of your children."

Nicholas pointed his finger at the woman. "Five hundred dollars. Six months in jail."

"Your honor," the pony-tailed lawyer said, "my client volunteered for public service. You are condemning this struggling mother to hell."

Like a rock-star drummer high on Ecstasy, Nicholas shattered court decorum by battering his gavel. The women, including the court reporter, recoiled. Only the newcomer in the back did not flinch.

Nicholas jabbed his finger toward the lawyer as if poking her from a distance. "Even a loud breath emitted from you and I'll increase your client's jail time to prison time."

While exiting toward his chambers, Nicholas avoided glancing at the backrow woman, but sensed her glazed-over eyes piercing the back of his scalp.

Nicholas shed his robe, changed into jogging clothes, and assured his hair was styled fashionably for navigating through the public.

He peeped into the courtroom. People had exited except for the woman in back who remained seated, leaning forward on her cane, focused upon the door through which Nicholas had exited.

Nicholas desired to avoid the woman, and yet, his curiosity, fascination, yearning, or some beckoning emotion drew him like a mosquito sensing heat of a pulsating artery. Was this strange woman a harbinger of news about his mother, a supporter of the condemned defendant, or perhaps an archangel carting ill tidings as depicted in grade-B sci-fi movies he often watched cloistered in his apartment?

He chuckled at his own fantastical imagination, envisioning himself as a superhero confronting a mythical demon in the back of his courtroom. His domain. His kingdom to protect.

He wiggled into his sixteen-year-old college varsity sweater, his guard against the outside world's springtime air—or, as he mused, wool armor shielding against other-worldly creatures masquerading in his court.

He valued his expansive imagination. An imagination he relied upon to remedy vacuous TV shows and ads that insulted human intelligence.

He marched through the courtroom to the woman. "Tell me who you are and why you intruded my courtroom."

The woman struggled to stand, holding up her hand in gesture she would not accept help. Nicholas was surprised. He had thought of offering help but had not indicated such.

The woman's hand trembled with Parkinsonian swaying as she reached out and pressed the flat of her hand upon Nicholas's abdomen. She maintained it in place for several seconds, withdrew it, slid her hand beneath her loose cloak, and shuffling her feet, disappeared into the hallway.

Nicholas deliberated for a few seconds before stepping out from the courtroom. He was dumbstruck to find the length of the hall was empty.

3. THE JOURNEY HOME

Nicholas jogged from court-complex shade into sunlight illuminating Marshall Park, pausing to run in place beside ducks and geese splashing in the pond. Despite mid-city serenity of the green space, he could not shake feeling contaminated. The strange woman had violated him. Laid her hand on his very private belly. Leaving him feeling soiled, penetrated.

Nonsense, he thought. A silly, little woman who could barely see or walk, feeling her world to gain knowledge that her eyes failed to capture. Her touching him must be an adaption of being blind.

And yet ...

He fast-walked along Third-Street toward Charlotte's uptown. His rented suite above a museum lay nine blocks from the courthouse. He preferred walking, and in fact, cherished walking. He frequently altered routes, sometimes circling the Charles R. Jones Federal Building, home of a US District Court. Old postcards showed the building surrounded by rows of imperial trees, but after the ISIS attack on the New York World Trade Center, trees surrounding government buildings were sacrificed to eliminate lairs for terrorists ambushing lawyers, politicians, or civil servants. Marshall Park across from his court was a pleasant exception.

He yearned to work in a venerable venue such as the Jones Building. Important cases. Cases in the spotlight. Years before, behind that building's august Doric columns, General David Petraeus, a CIA Director, was declared guilty of disclosing classified information to his mistress.

But today, Nicholas chose the quickest route to escape the legal arena and nestle in the solace of his thirty-seventh-floor apartment, change into swimwear, jog up steps to the rooftop, dive into the forty-second-floor, salt-water pool, and swim laps as he did in college with the Davidson Wildcats, proving to the universe he was master of the breaststroke.

His breaststroke had won him a full scholarship, opened doors to attend a prestigious school, and provided climbing social ladders. His climb, however, crumpled due to his aversion to socializing and inability to form lasting relationships. Rather than sulk over his aberrant childhood, he patted himself on the back for not only surviving, but being on track for ascending the legal ranks.

While passing the Charlotte Mecklenburg Government Center housing a local-chain restaurant serving Greek food inauthentic enough it would have tortured his mother, he spotted the backside of the elderly blind woman. She was sitting across the street in a wheelchair, alone beneath an oak on the First Baptist Church grounds. She appeared to be tossing seeds onto well-trimmed grass where an abundance of birds had flocked.

Could she see the birds? Hear them?

Rather than proceed to the crosswalk, he jaywalked and skulked through the grass like a sniper cautious to not alert his target.

Without turning around, the woman asked, "Are you following me?"

Nicholas listened, confirming traffic clatter was loud enough to have obscured his steps. "How do you know someone is standing behind you?"

"How is it you assume to know the lives of the people you judge?"

Nicholas scanned the area for mirrors or shiny objects betraying his identity. "How do you know I'm a judge?"

The woman chuckled.

Nicholas inhaled deeply, embittered by the woman behaving as if she were a carnival mystic. "I happen to know people's lives because I have skills at seeing what most people fail to see."

"Ah yes," the woman said. "You and I have that gift—or curse. Seeing what others cannot."

Nicholas eased to the front side of the woman. "My mother warned me I dangerously exceeded at reading people."

"Did you believe her?"

"Believe my mother?" Nicholas huffed. "Hardly."

The woman leaned forward and jammed her cane into the earth. "When the gods bless us, we are obligated to use our bestowal for the good of humankind." She jabbed the ground again.

Nicholas startled at his elder's fierce move. "And do you, yourself, act for the good of humankind?"

The woman's head bobbled long enough for Nicholas to think she must be reviewing a century of life.

Finally, she mumbled, "I do. When I am able to see far enough ahead."

Nicholas felt self-conscious, hoping no one from work saw him talking to a strange lady in a wheelchair feeding birds. "I do not believe my foreknowledge is a gift—or curse."

The woman raised her voice is if scolding Nicholas. "Acknowledgement keeps us on the path."

Nicholas took a knee beside the woman. "Why did you touch my belly?"

"I wasn't certain you noticed."

"Bullshit. You know I noticed."

The woman looked to the heavens. "Creatures climb into others' hearts to revere what is there."

Nicholas stood and shuffled his feet like an anxious child standing in line, praying to not be the last player selected for a team. "Tell me why you touched me."

"Why does one touch anything? Anyone? All things come to fruit."

Nicholas felt irritated by the woman's riddles. He surveyed the area, checking if they were being observed. "I don't know what the fuck your riddles mean, old woman."

The woman struggled wheeling her chair forward.

Nicholas thought of offering help, but a reluctance to become further entangled won out. He yelled, "Will you be coming around again?"

"I seek out those who are worthy."

An SUV pulled into the church drive. A man wearing a 1940's suit stepped out and aided the woman across the lawn and into the vehicle's back seat.

Nicholas called out to the man. "What's her name?"

The man remained stoic and silent until he had stored the chair in back. "What do you wish to call her?"

Nicholas whispered beneath his breath, "More goddamn riddles," followed by alarm he had cursed on a church's sacred grounds.

As the man approached the driver's door, Nicholas yelled louder. "How often does she come here to feed the birds?"

"She does not feed the birds. The birds watch. She seeds the lawn."

The man nodded good day and drove away.

Nicholas felt chilled. More than a sunny, springtime day should feel.

4. A REVEALING SWIM

Enough weeks passed for Nicholas to have adjudicated dozens of cases. Today, like all court days, parties had been enraged by his judgments, a climate he gladly abandoned for the tranquility and beach smell of his tower's salt-water pool.

He initiated his rooftop workout by dangling his feet in the water, adjusting his googles, and looking upward toward an office skyscraper jutting twenty stories higher than his pool.

Despite a crippling office vacancy following the Covid epidemic, Nicholas assumed someone must be working in the monolithic tower. Perhaps a nosy office worker with binoculars was zooming in on him. Perhaps office workers were placing bets on his time. His time never varied more than twenty seconds. His spying fans would know to bet within a tight range.

He always donned Speedos. Perhaps a voyeur or two were aroused by his magazine-worthy physique. In college, he had experienced observers hitting on him post meets. Both women and men. Even a couple of underaged girls who had embraced everything possible to look older.

Dating had never been his forte—slamming doors shut on romance and sex.

Once, when his dormmates got him intoxicated severely enough that he lapsed into an almost-coma and stopped breathing, the young men freaked out. One, a football lineman, performed a mouth-to-mouth maneuver. After being revived, Nicholas asked everyone the same question, "While drunk, did I get laid?" All answered, "Shit yeah." He assumed they were lying—hoped they were lying. It would suck to not remember his first time.

Sitting on the edge of the pool, Nicholas glanced down

at his abdomen, his habit to assure he was maintaining tight muscles and had no fat pads. But he detected a bulge. This morning, his bathroom scales had registered a couple of pounds heavy. He attributed the rare increase to having splurged on a piece of coconut-cream pie. Surely, he had worked that off by fast-walking to and from work and jogging up thirty-seven flights upon return to his manor in the sky.

When he rubbed the area below his belly button, he felt a lump. Holy shit.

He stood to examine his belly. Even standing, he detected the lump. He knew of no family history of cancer, but then again, the only family he had known was his mother. She had been a dramatic hypochondriac who even thought her knuckles had malignancies.

Suppressing a smirk, he had once suggested she get her knuckles CAT scanned, inciting her to appear on the verge of vomiting. "God no. Everyone who is radiated by those machines gets cancer."

He thought, Maybe this lump is merely a muscle knot and if I swim it will go away. If not, then I'll take action.

There had been worries over the years for which during and after swimming, he enjoyed amnesia. He appreciated that about himself. Came in handy dealing with criminal acts: pillaging, plundering, date raping, spraying illegal graffiti, and rare cases of murder.

As he slow-kicked his dangling legs in the pool, he relived college days of grandstands cheering as he stood enswathed with confidence. His swims were always great. His world would become silent. Spectators and natatorium noises would fade. The only sound would be his heart beating. The other lanes, the room, all would become black as if suspended in outer space. In his mind, only his lane appeared illuminated as if by a solo light.

This afternoon, Nicholas's lone rooftop swim was

equally magnificent as he settled into oneness with the cosmos. The sun, a sliver of moon, the heavens all celebrated his graceful ballet of the water world.

After completing his Olympic feat, he performed a push-up on the concrete-block rim and leapt to his feet in a well-rehearsed gymnastic move.

He had indeed forgotten his unwelcomed lump, but as he dried off, he rediscovered the smooth curvature of a deformity within his gut. Fuck. What is that? He looked around. There was no one to notice. No one to approach for a second opinion—not that he ever would.

He hurried inside, skipped the stairs, took the elevator, and rushed to his full-length bedroom mirror. He could see the lump. It was like a billiard ball buried beneath thick covers, pushing upward to form a smooth dimple. What was inside him? His stomach? Intestines? He had felt vague discomfort in that area during the night. When he got up to urinate in the middle of the night—an unusual event for him—he desired to vomit. Spill out something inside him that should not be there. Baked beans that stalled in his gut? Usually, beans agreed with him. Milk? The glass he guzzled before bed faintly smelled soured. Perhaps the sensation was a strained muscle. That happened in college the one time he attempted weight lifting.

Should he get checked out? But doctors always manage to find the last thing you want to hear. Oh God. He was sounding like his mother. Shit. Anyone but that contrary crock.

An afflicting memory erupted. He once boasted to his kindergarten class during show-and-tell that Eleni was not actually his mother, but was a notorious criminal who kidnapped him as an infant.

After his teachers informed his mother, he prepared to be horse-whipped or burned at the stake. But Eleni only stared at him for an eternity, never broaching the topic.

He obsessed that his mother's silence signified he had tapped into the tip of an iceberg of family horrors. Why else would she repeatedly tell him cruel stories of retribution by the goddess Nemesis punishing hubris, and the god Cronus swallowing his newborn children?

In the fourth grade, he pleaded for a Batman outfit, determined to protect himself from his wicked caregiver, seek out his real parents, and stand for "Truth, Justice, and the American Way."

His classmate Lowell had humiliated him in front of gym class, broadcasting that Nicholas bragged he was the true Batman and was destined to become the next Derek Jeter of baseball. "But you've all seen Nicholas, right? The worst batter and catcher in our school. More pathetic than first-grade girls." Lowell did not stop there. He shouted to his gathering audience, "Nicholas is a geek. The moron mixes up Superman's creed with his lame hero Batman."

All the classmates gave the thumbs-up sign and jeered.

That afternoon, Nicholas tossed his Batman costume and Derek Jeter draft-pick baseball card into his mother's attic to be consumed by his mother's illimitable cornucopia.

Batman and Derek had been important childhood friends, but he had coldly discarded them to the spiders and webs of the attic. Maybe they were now rising from the ashes and seeking revenge. Strapping him with a belly mass.

Nicholas's childlike ruminating of miseries halted when two young women emerged from the rooftop lounge, nursing beers with the brands obscured by foam-rubber holders. Beer was bearable, but Nicholas hoped the women weren't smokers. Nothing turned him off faster.

Both were well-tanned. Maybe they had just returned from a cruise. He hoped that they had not toasted themselves in tanning beds. That would guarantee they were diseased.

One woman waved with subminimal finger-flapping, signaling, we recognize your presence—whoever you are—but don't approach or talk to us.

Not that he desired to talk with them. If he resumed swimming, he could avoid their diatribes about dating hopefuls, bridesmaid bar hopping, unfaithful ex-boyfriends, or woes of womanhood.

As he was submerging to push off the pool wall, he heard one woman mention genomic imprinting.

Wow. Maybe he had severely misjudged. Did not have the gods' gift or curse that the blind soothsayer elder had heralded.

Should he have followed the old hag's advice and looked into these women's hearts? But doing so would risk unmasking the women's excessive heartaches. He had managed to skirt through life and never inquire about his mother's perpetual frown.

He surrendered to the graceful rhythms of dancing with water as all things of mind and earth evanesced.

5. THE EXAM

An internist in a lengthy white coat entered the exam room, followed by a medical scribe rolling a mobile workstation. "Hi. I'm Dr. Juliana Epione from internal medicine."

Nicholas locked eyes on Juliana's nametag, feeling wary a young, foreign, woman physician would be assessing him. While she washed her hands in the miniature sink, he asked, "Where are you from?"

"Pardon me?"

"Where are you from? Where did you grow up?"

"Oh … Akron, Ohio. Where did you grow up?"

"Chicago."

"Ah." Juliana smiled. "I spent holidays visiting my grandparents in Chicago. Great city. Now I—"

"Where were they from?"

Having a surname unfamiliar to many patients, Juliana recognized Nicholas's game and was agreeable to play along. "Who?"

"Your grandparents?"

"Chicago."

"I mean before that."

"Deerfield. Outside Chicago."

"What kind of name is Epione?"

"My grandfather told me his own grandfather had relatives from Italy, Sicily—somewhere in that region. What is your family history?"

"Greek I was led to believe."

Juliana raised an eyebrow. "Led to believe?"

"My mother was an incessant story teller. She loved to fabricate. So, I believe but am not certain."

"Have you visited Greece?"

Nicholas stared at the floor like a shamed pet dog.

"Hope to someday."

"Anything else you would like to know?"

"Where did you attend medical school?"

"Northwestern University. Chicago. Anything else?"

"All sounds good."

"Glad I passed your inspection. Now then, tell me about why you're here."

"My mother had all young, foreign doctors in Chicago. She died recently."

The reason Nicholas had grilled her became clear for Juliana. "I see. I'm sorry to hear about your loss."

They sat in silence for a long moment as the scribe scrolled through computer information.

Nicholas broke the silence. "I have a lump."

"Okay."

He indicated his lower abdomen. "It appeared maybe five, six weeks ago. I should have come in sooner."

"Is it painful?"

"More like uncomfortable."

"Associated with other symptoms?"

"I had a bout of nausea early on, but that could have been my imagination. Happens the rare times I'm anxious."

"What do you think the lump is?"

"I worry it is cancerous."

"Any recent trauma, injuries?"

"None."

"Over-exertion?"

"I swim forty laps every day, jog several miles, race up steps to my thirty-seventh-floor apartment."

"Goodness. You are in good shape."

"Try to eat healthily."

"Any medications?"

"Vitamin C and zinc when I think I'm catching a cold."

"Changes in bowel movements?"

"No."

"Blood in your urine?"

Nicholas shook his head no.

"Can you hop on the table, lie back, and let me examine you?"

"Sure." Nicholas gracefully pirouetted to the table top and stretched back with arms resting behind his scalp.

"And pull up your shirt."

"Oh. Of course." Nicholas rolled up his shirt to reveal his abdomen, watching to see if his physique impressed the internist, a woman he assessed as being in her late twenties. He thought, She's obviously trained to maintain an expressionless face. Like I attempt to do in court.

"Which side?"

"In the center."

Juliana slipped on surgical gloves. "Pardon the cold room. Our AC has been in overdrive." She gently percussed his abdomen. "Let me know if anything feels tender or painful." She tapped several times, massaged the area of interest, and listened with her stethoscope. At last, her face demonstrated an emotion: concern.

Nicholas's forehead furrowed. "You felt it, didn't you?"

"You definitely have something in your pelvic area. Firm. Not sharp, jagged, or hard. Evenly rounded. Normal bowel sounds. Let's get a urine sample and some blood work. We should get a look at whatever that is. An abdominal x-ray. Look at your liver, spleen, stomach, intestines. A KUB x-ray for kidneys, ureters, bladder. See what we're dealing with."

While waiting for results in the radiology waiting area, Nicholas snacked on types of candy and crackers he usually avoided, and doodled in hospital-magazine margins, scrawling cartoon characters of a lion wrestling a python.

Dr. Epione's assistant entered. "Mr. Charon? Dr.

Epione is ready for you in the consultation room."

Nicholas wanted to instruct the assistant to address him as Judge Charon, but as they walked along the hall, he capitulated that this was a medical arena, not his turf. But still, he ached to instruct the assistant to wear more than surgery pajamas. Pajamas made him feel awkward as if he had intruded upon a half-dressed person climbing out of bed.

Juliana continued staring at x-rays as she talked, unaware if Nicholas was standing or sitting until she sensed him breathing near her ear and overlooking her shoulder. She pointed at the image. "This is what we found. A fluid-filled cyst-like structure. The good news is that cysts are not typically cancerous. It's good news that the cyst is uniform. A biopsy will tell us for sure. We can schedule that for later this week. In the meantime, we should perform a CT scan today for additional data."

"So, not a tumor?"

"Tumors are masses of abnormal cells. More solid. Cysts are filled with fluid or air. Your cyst is in your pelvis, but not infiltrating your bladder or kidneys. Your liver, stomach, intestines all appear fine."

She turned to Nicholas. "Let's do that CT scan and schedule a biopsy."

Once Nicholas left the room, Juliana pointed at the x-ray, highlighting the cyst for her assistant. "Almost resembles a uterus, doesn't it? But I wonder what it is."

6. TEAM WORK

After Nicholas left the clinic, Juliana ordered a thorough reading of the CT scan, consulting a radiologist, Dr. Aaron Badalich.

She had seen Aaron a few times in the halls and once playing volleyball at a hospital picnic, estimating he was in his early thirties.

They sat in roller chairs as Aaron pointed at images. "Here's the cyst you felt, a sac that's barely conspicuous on x-ray. More interesting is this smaller 2.5 cm unilocular cyst with a thick, crenulated, enhancing wall. At first, I thought it was a submucosal fibroid, but we'll come back to that."

Juliana leaned closer. "And the larger cyst I felt on exam?"

"It's fluid-filled as you described from the x-ray, but see this eccentric curvilinear structure at the periphery of the sac? In women, that could be interpreted as the beginning of a placenta."

"Placenta?" Juliana shoved her chair back from the monitor. "That doesn't make sense."

"I'm sure it will turn out to be something else, but who knows exactly what? I'm just saying this area oddly resembles early cells of a placenta in a uterus."

"In a man?"

"A uterus would be highly unusual in a man but not unheard of. Look closer at the larger cyst you palpated."

Juliana rolled closer as Aaron indicated with the tip of his laser pointer. "Three layers. A well-defined inner endometrium zone. A hypointense, poorly marginated junctional zone. And here is an outer intermediate intensity myometrium. Remarkably like a uterus."

Although their language was academic as are many

medical consultations, casual observers would have guessed the two animated physicians were discussing plans for an evening rendezvous.

Aaron slid his laser pointer lower. "And down here. A vaginal-like structure extending from the uterus-like structure, but ending nowhere—so to speak. Where's the fun in that, huh?"

Juliana huffed with a forced grin at Aaron's attempt at humor and leaned within inches of the monitor. "I suspected it resembled a uterus, but I wasn't about to dictate that in my differential."

Aaron highlighted another portion of the scan. "Now back to that little 2.5 cm cyst. I ran that past two colleagues. That cyst resembles a co-existing ovarian corpus luteum. As strange as it sounds, I'd check out that structure to see if it's producing progesterone."

"Like in early pregnancy?" Juliana stood and backed away. "I feel like I'm in a weird nightmare. Men have none of that plumbing."

"Only three hundred cases of a uterus in a man ever reported. The Persistent Mullerian Duct Syndrome. Such patients have normal male reproductive organs, but also have a uterus and fallopian tubes. The result of an autosomal recessive disorder not dissolving those structures that are present in all fetuses prior to sex differentiation."

Juliana pressed her back against a wall as if holding back a destructive beast determined to plow into her world of certainty. "Do we trust these images enough to dare present such a hypothesis to our patient?"

Aaron pondered a moment. "May I suggest forming a team of you, a radiologist—me if you wish—a gynecologist, perhaps a psychiatrist would be helpful—maybe even a chaplain?"

"Good God." Juliana buried her face in her hands. "I

shouldn't have gotten out of bed this morning and put in my contacts. Remaining blind would have suited me better."

Aaron strolled to the despondent internist. "Come on now. Where's your sense of adventure?"

Juliana smirked. "At least you didn't recommend someone from the press to round out a gigantic team."

"You know news like this will spread like wildfire—no matter what safeguards we employ. How is this man—?" Aaron interrupted himself. "He does live as a man, correct?"

Juliana pursed her lips. "A fragile, unpleasant, insecure, sometimes hostile, condescending human being. A man."

"Be kind, Dr. Epione." Aaron grinned, having heard of his colleague's propensity for quips about male patients.

As Juliana drove home, she whispered to herself multiple times. "A man with a uterus. That I can believe. A stretch, but possible. Nature plays tricks. But a pregnancy? Not even nature would do that."

A few miles closer to home, she slapped the palm of her hand on the steering wheel. "If there is something there, it's got to be a hormone-laden tumor."

And a moment later, "Absolutely not a pregnancy."

7. WHY ME?

During the nights following the biopsy and being informed of his diagnosis—that of having a uterus—Nicholas could not sleep. All he could dwell on was, "I have a womb inside me. A goddamn fucking woman womb."

Nicholas squirmed with ruthless obsessing befogging clarity as much as a cloud of stink bugs splattering on his windshield.

It had not helped that half of the time the team said, "uterus-like structure," and the other half simply, "uterus."

How could he go this far in life and not know? But then again, he had never been subjected to an abdominal x-ray. The most he had experienced was a wrist x-ray following a collision when a rival swimmer crossed into his lane. And that was ancient history, far back, twenty years ago in high school.

Had others recognized something had been off about him? In his teens, kids poked fun of his immaculate grooming and dressing habits. At home, late at night in his bedroom, he frequently browsed through copies of *GQ Magazine* for fashion ideas, attracted to the finest clothing. Or was something else attracting him? Shit. Had he been titillated by the models? He could not deny he enjoyed their looks. But did being attracted even a tiny bit signify he was gay? Or was it more than that? Was it because deep inside, he was actually part woman?

Holy fuck. Had his brain been commandeered with effeminate thinking because some goddamn part of him was part woman? Shit.

What could he possibly do? There's not one human on the face of the earth to whom he would dare revel this secret—no. Not some secret. But a cruel-joke deformity about which multiple medical types were likely spreading the news across Charlotte and beyond.

Perhaps, he had always known. He had never been interested in dating. Now it was clear. How do you date when you are two fucking sexes?

Oh God, he thought. No wonder I can't sleep. I've always had depressing, haunting, torturing dreams. And now knowing this? If I go to sleep, raging nightmares will nuke me.

I might as well have been informed I am half-human, half-horse. An oddity like my mother's Greek mythical creatures. Or informed I am a werewolf. Human by day and some crap thing at night. Maybe sprout fangs. No. Something worse. Sprout a uterus.

Nicholas was frightened to touch his belly and feel the thing inside him, acknowledge the curse entombed inside him.

Suddenly, he had a revelation.

The woman on the backrow.

The mystic hag overflowing with riddles outside the church.

The invasive sorceress who had invaded his belly.

This is her doing.

Dr. Epione told me, "Congenital." But what if I were not born with a uterus? What if this condition is new?

But I would be locked away if I suggested that witchery is involved. I would be tossed into a dungeon and shot up with tiger or elephant tranquilizers.

Or maybe my mother is playing with my body from heaven—or the underworld—wherever that spiteful woman ended up.

What did I ever do to her? ... Well, lots actually—but if this is her retaliation, what she chose is far, far out of bounds.

The man in court screamed, "Burn in hell," but dozens of defendants screamed that curse and I never had my body or mind assaulted with venomous retribution.

That's exactly what this is. Retribution.

Do I deserve this? Absolutely not. I'm not an evil person. I treat people fairly. People just don't always appreciate "fairly."

There's not a thing I would change about myself. People should laud me for striving for perfection. Sure, I may have flaws. Little flaws like undertipping. Scowling when street people beg. Or crying babies in restaurants. Oh my God. Babies crying in restaurants are the worst. A few times—not all that many—I lifted and slammed my plate onto my table while glaring at their parents. But I was justified. Those parents deserved to be reminded that other people are paying good money to dine in peace—that I was paying good money to dine in peace.

Are those flaws? Maybe. Maybe not. But not to the degree to have the universe install a uterus inside me.

Nicholas looked down at his feet poking out of the covers where he had tugged his bedding loose with his restless squirming.

"Oh God. Now what? Really? My ankles are swelling?"

8. HEAD SCRATCHING

Juliana and Aaron bonded while grappling with their patient's one-in-a-million condition, addressing one another by first names. It was like sharing an Indiana-Jones medical adventure. But after they performed a pregnancy test on Nicholas's urine, and his HcG levels came back confirming pregnancy, Nicholas evolved to being a one-in-eight-billion human.

Forget Indiana Jones. Juliana and Aaron were on a space flight to Jupiter's moons. The two physicians, however, had yet to welcome Nicholas aboard their space craft to discuss the newest finding.

Juliana's coffee went cold as she stared at a lab report, thinking, How do you devastate a human being by informing him that he has the inside workings of two genders, and then follow-up with breaking-news that he also is bearing new life within his body?

Juliana and Aaron jointly agreed to restrict themselves to saying, "him" and "his" when talking about Nicholas, avoiding "she" and "her." Aaron abruptly learned to not use the pronoun "they" after Nicholas screamed at him for saying, "When a person has such a condition, they should—"

Aaron disliked Nicholas's personality enough that during after-work martinis with Juliana, he confessed that when discussing Nicholas, he preferred applying the pronoun "it."

Aaron also disliked that Nicholas fired his assigned psychiatrist. After listening to Nicholas tell his uninterrupted story for an hour, the psychiatrist made the mistake of saying, "I know exactly where you are coming from." Game over.

Although over the years a multitude of patients in the

clinic had yelled at caregivers delivering ill-timed information, Nicholas's eruption had been akin to Wellington personally meeting Napoleon at Waterloo and proclaiming, "You're even much shorter than British propaganda led me to believe."

War ensued in the clinic, requiring security and a psychiatric team to rush to the scene and threaten to use restrains and force sedatives.

One security guard loudly stated, "That's the S.O.B. who granted custody of my children to my deranged, drug-addict wife. May he rot in hell. Let me jab him with the needle."

Nicholas filed a formal complaint against that guard and the entire clinic staff. As a result, the CEO of the managing parent company of the hospital called a meeting.

The CEO, Christian Beckett, sat at the head of the table. "Can someone please explain to me how a man—the first in history other than a handful of transgender men—or women—or whatever—could be pregnant?"

The gynecologist on the team, Dr. Ruby Rose, answered. "We have several theories, all of them tenuous. None verifiable. Just suppositions. So, that—"

"So, cutting to the short of it, you know absolutely nothing."

Dr. Rose's facial contortions resembled an infant straining to have a bowel movement as she yearned for an answer—any answer to materialize.

"Is he gay?" Mr. Beckett asked.

Dr. Rose stuttered. "That ... that could not possibly explain ... there's no way ... for physical impregnation to occur ... even if he had ... with another man."

"What are you suggesting? He swallowed watermelon seeds? Self-impregnated?"

Members of the team played pass-the-hot-potato with

glances at one another for a long minute until Juliana fielded the inquiry. "There's no way for sperm from this man's testes to get to his uterus—if that really is a uterus."

Mr. Beckett heaved a sigh. "You stated earlier it truly is a uterus. That is what you clearly informed me on the phone."

"I did. Apologies. However, there's no physical route for sperm … to get there much less implant."

"And yet here we are."

Juliana tapped her fingers on the table top. "We definitely are here."

Mr. Beckett circled the team, stopping behind the hospital chaplain. "Samuel? I haven't heard a word from you. Do you have anything to add?"

"Well," Reverend Samuel Forrest began, pausing to sip water and sniffle, "I met with Judge Charon twice for several hours. That poor soul has little capacity for listening. Once he began to open up, he was like a rambling, long-winded, dogmatic politician."

"Amen to that," Aaron whispered while rolling his eyes. Then suddenly, "I didn't mean amen like … amen, Reverend … just that I experienced the same impression of the judge. That's all I—"

"You're tripping over yourself, Dr. Badalich," Mr. Beckett said. "So, Samuel, you were saying—"

"I was saying this man half-heartedly—and I say half-heartedly because I believe this man would truly welcome a rational explanation, but this man—and I was taken aback by this—this man believes a demon or some kind of voodoo person placed a hex on him."

Everyone in the room fell silent, paralyzed as if suspended in a photo immortalizing the moment.

Samuel moved to standing behind the conference room's podium and hunching over as if ready to deliver a sermon. "I have eagerly been waiting for this panel of experts to offer a rational, scientific explanation for this man's condition. I've heard none. You claim there's a definite fetal heartbeat—but too early to see bone formation. And although you profess there is definitely a pregnancy, you doubted that the fetus would survive for long. But this miraculous life exceeded your predictions for limited longevity. Does it really matter how it got here? Self-fertilization? Demons or voodoo? Immaculate conception?"

"What?" Mr. Beckett screamed. "The last thing we need, Samuel, is to additionally turn this medical nightmare into a religious fiasco."

"A living fetus in a uterus—or uterus-like structure as some of you insist—is most definitely life. And life, my good colleagues, is unequivocally a religious issue."

"This isn't life," Mr. Beckett yelled. "This is a freakish mistake of nature. If this thing is allowed to grow, it has no way to come out naturally. If it dies, it has no way to be expelled."

The chaplain clasped his hands and lowered his voice as monks do when signaling they are treading gently. "Maybe it's not a freak of nature," Samuel muttered softly enough that everyone leaned closer. "Maybe what it is, is a divine gift of nature."

"Oh my … golly," Mr. Beckett screamed.

Juliana scooted her chair back hard enough that it screeched. She stood and leaned forward with hands propped on the table as if pinning it to the earth. "I can't believe we are having this conversation. This will become a life-threatening medical situation for this man. It's not like this is some 'immaculate conception.'"

"Maybe not," Samuel said, "but Judge Charon assured me he is a virgin—and I believe him. Therefore, this will be—at the least—a virgin birth."

Aaron scooted his chair back with even more force, toppling it backwards. "I don't believe for a second this man is a virgin. I don't believe this man is a saint. He throws gravel at puppies that bark when he jogs past them. He turned in a second-grader for selling cookies in his building's lobby without a license."

"How do you know that?" Juliana asked.

"We had this guy flat on his back rolling him into the scan. He never stopped talking. He has no filter, no self-restraint. He brags of superhero fantasies. Doodled little-kid cartoons in our waiting-room magazines. This guy's nothing but a child in a judge's robe."

Christian Beckett wiped a bead of sweat from his brow, placed his hand on Samuel's shoulder, and whispered, "You haven't mentioned this virgin thing—this virgin birth idea—to anyone, have you, Samuel?"

Samuel shrugged.

"Good Lord, Samuel. You know there's no such thing as a secret in this clinic. If you blab to people that this man's condition is some kind of miracle, it will leak to the public and explode like Covid across social media."

"I didn't tell anyone, Christian. I felt obligated to share my thinking with you here in this room. That's the extent of it."

Mr. Beckett turned to Dr. Allison Petri, the newly recruited replacement psychiatrist joining the team. "Allison? We haven't heard from you. What does this patient say he believes happened?"

Dr. Petri stared at her notebook of handwritten scribbles. "Well ... even after I proposed a few tentative medical explanations, the patient—prefacing that he was sure his own personal theory would be dismissed by us as totally insane—told me—in confidence—that he thought a witch in the back of his court placed a spell on him. Grew a uterus in him."

Dr. Petri gently closed her notebook. "That's what the honorable judge believes."

Mr. Beckett sank back into a chair. "A witch grew him a uterus. Wow. Now I've heard everything—more than everything."

Mr. Beckett tapped his lips with his pencil as if it were a cigarette he craved to smoke. "And what is his theory about being pregnant?"

Everyone else in the room glanced numerous times at every other person except toward Mr. Beckett.

"What?" Mr. Beckett asked. "What's going on?"

Juliana broke the silent-stare game. "We haven't informed him he's pregnant."

Mr. Beckett sat up, propped his elbows on the conference table, and covered his eyes. "God help us all."

9. TAXES, DEATH, AND PREGNANCY

Worsening breast tenderness was not Nicholas's primary concern. Instead, he obsessed if anyone could notice his swollen breasts.

He began wearing a T-shirt when swimming, however, upon viewing himself in a clubhouse mirror, he realized his wet T-shirt clung to him like plastic wrap around left-over potato salad, accentuating his nipples.

He purchased a wetsuit jacket. Modeling the jacket in the mirror, he was satisfied, but during his swim, he suffered neoprene effacing his nipples with the force of medieval torture.

He purchased wetsuit boots to conceal his swelling ankles, but they crushed his feet. He purchased shoes two sizes larger to accommodate his puffy feet, causing him to frequently stumble.

And his appetite? Voracious. For decades, he had a dietary routine of a yogurt-and-coffee breakfast, a lunch snack of crackers and cheese, and a reasonable size dinner of various fish, spinach-kale salads, a serving of a vegetable such as broccolini, and if his weight held steadily, he banqueted on a whole-wheat roll lathered in butter. Dessert was a once-a-week treat with dark chocolate being mandatory.

He remembered how as a law clerk he once gained three pounds. For the following fortnight, he limited dinners to applesauce until discovering his scales were malfunctioning.

But this week, his scales registered a four-pound gain. He pruned his diet. Not only did he endure hunger, he had gluttonous nightmares of being marooned in a sun-blistering desert, drooling while ogling and smelling steaks, avocados, and banana splits perpetually beyond reach.

Nicholas surveyed the internet and learned that increased appetite can be associated with cancer, especially breast cancer. After coupling that science with having swollen, tender breasts, he scoured the internet for medical research articles, learning that one out of a hundred breast cancer cases occur in men.

He became so obsessed and overwhelmed with his breasts and pelvic bulge, that he muddled the histories of two defendants, mistakenly tongue-lashing a car thief for being the pervert who had exposed his genitals to a senior-citizen women's group rehearsing church choir.

He demanded the hospital page Dr. Epione. "I've been researching New England Journal articles. I need you to be honest and tell me if I have cancer. I have the symptoms of swollen breasts, of increased appetite, of—"

Juliana interrupted. "Can you come into the clinic?"

"What? Are you incapable of giving me a straight answer on the phone? You charge enough we should be communicating by telepathy."

"Some discussions are better in person."

"So, you are leading me to believe I have cancer, but you refuse to say it." He yelled, "I have a right to hear it from your mouth and immediately."

"I want you to come in."

"I handle bad news. I dish out bad news in court right and left. Let me have it."

Juliana retained a calming voice. "Please come in."

"This uterus-like thing is cancerous? Isn't it? And it's screwing up my hormone levels. Right?"

"Partially."

"Partially? What the hell does 'partially' mean?"

There was a silence lengthy enough that Nicholas chewed at a hangnail until it bled. Following Juliana's lead, he governed his speech to be at the level of a whisper. "I already believe I have cancer. Possibly, probably fatal. I need to know how much time I have left. I'm calm. I'm prepared. Let me have it."

After another lengthy pause, Juliana said, "All I can tell you is that you have a complex condition that we don't understand. We are perplexed. You and I—you and our team—need to put our heads together to come up with a plan. Please come in."

"I don't want to meet with your bubblehead team. I'll meet with you. Nobody else in the room. Not even your typing person—stenographer whatever. Those are my terms."

After a long pause, Juliana consented.

Nicholas pulled out a binder and reviewed a ruling on a case similar to one of his present cases. At conclusion, he remembered nothing of the ruling. He reread the ruling. And then read it again. And then could not recall why he was even reviewing that ruling.

10. TRUTH AND CONSEQUENCES

Juliana canceled her late afternoon patients to accommodate Nicholas.

Entering the exam room, Juliana was bewildered to see Nicholas pacing in a loose, shaggy sweater on a day of record-high heat. "Thank you for agreeing to come in."

"Thank you for honoring my request, for not beating around the bush more than you already have. Do I have cancer?"

Juliana gestured for them both to sit. "We have run numerous tests."

"A shit load."

"Yes. Numerous tests."

"And?"

"And we found no sign of cancer."

Nicholas stared out the clinic window at sun lighting a magnolia tree, the first moment he grasped the beauty of the day. His body felt more relaxed—relieved.

And yet …

Something felt wrong. Like the time his mother told him that she brought home the puppy he had adored in their neighborhood pet shop. The one he had named Boots because of its four white paws. After he had bounced up and down rejoicing, his mother added that the shop later called to inform her the puppy and its littermates tested positive for parvovirus and must be put to sleep. She had returned Boots.

Nicholas turned to Juliana, his face displaying apprehension. "What aren't you telling me?"

"You know—are accepting—you have a highly rare condition of a man having a uterus."

"I wouldn't use the word 'accepting.' Maybe 'surviving.' I'm doing my best to bury the uterus idea in my Victorian attic trunk."

"You're what?"

"I'm trying to ignore this abhorrent anomaly, but my body reminds me every moment I breathe or move."

"I want you to prepare yourself. Your condition is even rarer than we first believed."

"You're scaring me."

"Should I call Chaplain Samuel to join us?"

"Should I pluck off a testicle? The thought of having that pompous cleric join us constricts my rectal muscles."

"Anyone else you would like to be with you when I tell you?"

"Cut the fucking world's-best-sympathizer crap and tell me."

"You are pregnant."

Juliana had rehearsed in her mind possible reactions of yelling, cursing, threatening, name-calling, truth dismissing, and a host of typical patient reactions to bad news. She had not prepared for Judge Charon to pass out before he even had time to inhale, face-plant onto the tile floor, break his nose, and bleed profusely enough to look like a body riddled with gunshot.

She called a code and a multitude of staff members rushed in, including Aaron, Samuel, and Mr. Beckett who had been waiting in the hall, on-call if Juliana needed them. They stared at the body laid out in a pool of expanding blood as the code team jumped into action.

Mr. Beckett yelled, "She killed him."

"He's not dead, Christian," Aaron said. "She probably clobbered him like our entire team has been craving to do."

Nicholas's team sighted Juliana huddled in the corner with hands pressed to her temples, feeling guilty and thinking, I did not clobber him, but my words surely did.

A medical resident yelled to the enlarging crowd, "He

has a good pulse and is breathing fine."

Mr. Beckett exited the room, mumbling, "Shit. I smell a gargantuan lawsuit."

Samuel clutched the St. Christopher hanging from his neck. "I pray his unborn child survives this trauma."

Several staff members overheard Samuel and frowned, looking at one another as if to ask, "Did the chaplain really say what it sounded like he said?"

11. RECOVERY ROOM BLUES

Although Nicholas winced to painful stimuli, the emergency team was unable to arouse him.

Departing the room, one EMT whispered, "He's no longer unconscious. More like he refuses to wake up."

Aaron whispered to Juliana, "A spoiled child not wanting to go to school."

"Which school?" Juliana mumbled.

"Adult school of reality."

"I hear you," Nicholas said, still not opening his eyes.

"Ah. The judge rises." Aaron approached the transfer stretcher. "How's your nose?"

"Same as my tits. Burning like hornet stings."

"And humor too. Your brain is recovering higher functions."

Nicholas exhaled, sounding like a kid's squeezed beach float deflating.

"Please forgive me." Juliana eased closer. "You demanded I let you have it."

"I was expecting a slap, at worst a punch. Not a sledge hammer." Nicholas opened his eyes and squinted as he struggled to focus on his two physicians. "Any chance I'm dreaming what you said?"

Aaron sat on a stool, matching head levels with Nicholas. "Do you want me to also say it? Or do you want Dr. Epione to repeat herself?"

"I don't want any mortal to ever say it. Shit. How is … is … what you said … even possible?"

Juliana scooted a chair closer and sat. "We racked our brains for scientific explanations. We came up empty."

Nicholas inhaled and exhaled several deep breaths, flinching from nose pain. "Maybe the answer's not scientific."

"Our chaplain attempted to explain your condition, saying—"

"I don't give a rat's ass what that stiff-collared, man-of-the cloth thinks. He's incapable of original thought. His brain is junked with memorized moronic phrases."

"Didn't think you would be interested," Aaron mumbled.

"Thank you, Doctor … Doctor uh … Doctor Radiology."

"Badalich."

"Dr. Badalich. It's probably no shock if I confess to you that I was the first—likely the only eight-year-old in the history of St. Patrick's—to fail Sunday School."

"What did you do?"

"I substituted bourbon for the communion wine."

"Damn. I would have paid to watch that."

"I would have gotten away with it if Linus Douka's brother hadn't staggered to the altar rail a third time."

Aaron grinned at Juliana, conveying he was beginning to bond with the guy, but Juliana's stern frown was as good as a slap on the hand.

"So?" Juliana asked Nicholas, "What is your theory? It can't be wilder than our conjectures."

Nicholas pushed upward on his elbows and quickly fell back upon his pillow. "Still a bit dizzy."

"Could be the meds," Aaron said. "So?"

"So." Nicholas paused, thinking he was in the position of many defendants who had come before him, struggling between revealing truth or burying truth. "Did you ever feel something is absolutely true—even if it borders on magic or mythical—but in your gut it feels truthful, no matter how preposterous?"

Aaron smiled, warmed by a memory. "I only step up to bat if beneath my baseball jersey I'm wearing my father's dog tags. Once when my brother hid them, I refused to play or eat until Mom forced Quinn to dig them out of his underwear drawer and surrender them."

For the first time in a year or more, Nicholas chuckled. "Yeah. Kind of like that."

Juliana did not speak, but held up her wrist, revealing a multi-colored elastic band. She stretched it and let it snap back into place.

Nicholas chuckled again. "Yeah. You too, huh?"

Nicholas sat up just enough to support himself on his elbows and motioned for them to come closer as if he were about to spill a CIA secret. "An elderly-plus, hunched-over, blind lady invaded my courtroom. Sat on the backrow. Had nothing to do with the case—or who knows? Maybe everything. As I left the courtroom, stopping near her, she placed her hand flat on my stomach—pardon me—on my pelvic area. Why would a stranger do that, huh? I felt diseased ever since. My imagination, right? But here I am. Crazy? Sounds fucking off-the-deep-end to me, but I need to find that woman. More than I ever needed to find anyone. Reverse her spell. And even if you shoot me up with science's vilest meds, they won't obliterate these thoughts. Much less make ... make this ..." Nicholas could not say the word he was thinking, but patted his belly. "Make this go away."

"What would be her reason?" Juliana asked.

Nicholas snorted like a horse relaxing. "Maybe cause I'm an asshole twenty-four hours a day. A grownup who as a kid failed Sunday School."

"What do you want to do?" Juliana asked. "If we ignore this pregnancy, it could kill you."

"Please don't use that "P" word."

"What do you want?"

"Help me find my witch, my enchantress, my necromancer."

Aaron leapt up with the exuberance of a kid excited by a playmate's challenge. "Do you have clues of her whereabouts?"

Nicholas tightly shut his eyes. "She hinted that once I was worthy—whatever the hell that means—I might see her again."

Nicholas re-collapsed on the stretcher. "Probably depends on if I can quit being an asshole."

"Where do we start?" Aaron asked.

"What?" Nicholas sat up all the way up. "You would help me?"

Aaron patted his chest. "As long as I have my pop's dog tags under my shirt."

Juliana gave a thumbs up. "I'm in. Just don't let any of our colleagues know."

12. A TRIO ON AN ADVENTURE

When CEO Christian Beckett heard through the rumor mill of Juliana and Aaron's plan of surrender, he short-circuited a million brain neurons.

"What the fuck are you two thinking? We have clinics busting at the seams because of a physician-and-nurse shortage. And you're going on a snipe hunt with a loon?"

"What do you suggest we do?" the duo asked in synchrony.

Mr. Becket whined disappointment. "What amusement-park ride did you two climb on? This patient has a tumor."

"A pregnancy," Juliana said, crossing her arms like a disciplining schoolmarm.

"A tumor acting like fertilized material," Mr. Beckett corrected, spit flying with each emphasized word. "I'm no physician, but it's obvious this thing should be surgically yanked out like any malignancy."

Juliana's crossed arms squeezed one another with a wrestler's death-grip ferocity. "Our patient did not consent to surgery or invasive procedures. And may I remind you, if any patient knows his rights, it's a patient who is a judge—a trial judge. One who has a history of ruling in malpractice cases."

Mr. Beckett's face reddened as if his necktie had become a tightening noose. He highballed toward his office as if delivering an executive order of war from the President to Congress.

Aaron whispered to Juliana, "We never discussed treatments with Mr. Charon."

"Mr. Beckett doesn't know that."

Aaron grinned. "One of my med-school teachers once told me, 'It's not that women are evil, it's that they are strategic.'"

Juliana grinned. "Thank you, dear Aaron. I like that. I'm strategic."

Juliana and Aaron met Nicholas at the First Baptist Church, a block from the courthouse. Nicholas was wearing his judge's robe.

"I guess," Aaron said, "if surgeons can wear surgical pajamas in public, judges can wear robes, although it is record-breaking hot today."

Nicholas glanced around, checking if anyone was within hearing distance. "A loose robe hides my boobs."

Aaron's face flushed. "Enough said."

Juliana surveyed the church lawn. "All right then, where did you see this unusual lady?"

"In a wheelchair on the grass over there." Nicholas led his helpers to the spot.

Aaron studied the terrain. "And she was able to roll across this grass?"

"A few feet. A chauffeur arrived and rolled her to an SUV. The last I saw of her."

"What was she doing here?" Juliana asked.

"Tossing out seeds. Dozens of birds were standing here watching, but not eating or tampering with her seeds."

"That's creepy," Aaron said.

"It was like they were her pets—or disciples."

Juliana waved off a gnat targeting her brow for a sip of sweat. "And she said she'd find you, come to you?"

"Maybe if I was worthy. Wish me luck on that one." Nicholas used his hand as a visor to block the sun and as a shield to block his helpers' stares. "I read up on hysterical pregnancies. They come and go like magic."

Juliana's tone shifted to lecture mode. "Pseudocyesis. Often with hormonal changes, but those conditions—unlike your condition—have absolutely no radiological findings."

"So, this curse is not just in my mind?"

"Most definitely not."

"So, am I crazy?"

Although close in age, Aaron used his comforting-parent voice. "This situation is as crazy as it gets, but you, Judge Charon, are not crazy."

"So, not a nightmare, but full-blown reality."

Julian chose a similar sympathetic tone. "A complicated reality."

Nicholas bent over, picked up a seed, and examined it with a lack of intensity as do people when stalling. "Why are you two going out of your way to help me? You have busy schedules. I'm sure the hospital can't spare you. Why?"

"Your case is amazingly unique," Juliana said. "Although Dr. Badalich and I are both physicians, we are scientists, obnoxiously nosy people driven by curiosity."

"And," Aaron added, "we write papers and give lectures. You—as cold as it sounds—are a stunning discovery."

"Maybe," Nicholas said, "but it's more than that, isn't it?"

"What other motive could we possibly have?" Juliana asked.

Nicholas spoke to the ground. "I think you care."

Aaron waited until Nicholas looked his way and then winked. "We care about you. We care about many things. I cared about winning my boyhood baseball games. I cheer on the Charlotte Knights occasionally—always the Atlanta Braves. And I cheer on my patients and the folks on our teams helping them. What about you? Who do you cheer on?"

Nicholas moved to sitting on the native-stone rim of a church planter. "I don't."

Juliana joined Nicholas sitting. "Surely there's a team

or a person or a group you cheer on. People you've met in your court whom you wish to succeed."

Nicholas remained silent with a frown as fixed as a plastic Halloween mask. His silence answered Juliana's question.

Juliana and Aaron did not say it, but thought, This man is a lone survivor—a child-like lone survivor.

They basked in a moment of sunshine, a mild, comforting breeze, and a pause in traffic clangor.

The moment of grace was soon shattered.

13. REVERENDS AND THEIR FLOCKS

Nicholas pointed at the church's front door and screamed, "What is this? An ambush?"

Juliana and Aaron sighted Reverend Samuel standing on the church portico, speaking with a woman draped in a choir robe.

Aaron mumbled, "And we were having such a nice moment."

Samuel bid the woman farewell, spotted his three onlookers, and approached. "What do we have here? Three stray lambs in search of a church?"

"Is this your church?" Juliana asked.

Samuel laughed with vigor like someone at a party pressing for attention. "I am far too busy to preside over a church. I grew up in the First Baptist Church in Lexington, completed my masters of divinity in professional healthcare at Liberty University, and am now a member of this esteemed congregation, sometimes singing in the choir. Off key. Instead of twelve basic notes, I am fraught with twenty-three. Are you three sight-seeing, enjoying being out in the sun on this lovely day—perhaps seeking guidance?"

"Don't tell him," Nicholas said.

"Could be we were meant to meet," Samuel said. "The Lord works in mysterious ways."

Nicholas clinched his teeth. "So do Russian President Putin and Satan."

"I see." Samuel studied a distant dark cloud moving in from the west. "Looks like we're in for a storm. Well ... you three have a blessed day."

The three truth-seekers watched Samuel disappear onto Third Street.

Nicholas mumbled, "Listening to that man is like

having a dentist climb up my asshole to extract my teeth."

They watched a young girl about eight-or-nine-years-old dart out from the church. "Did you see which way Reverend Forrest went?"

Juliana pointed at the street. "He walked that direction."

"Oh," the girl muttered and opened her closed fist. "He left his ring on the piano."

Juliana leaned forward for a close look. "Gaelic markings. Very attractive. Does the reverend play piano?"

The girl made a face as if smelling rotting fish. "He tries to sing."

Aaron pinched the ring and held it to his eye. "Nice. We work with Reverend Forrest at our hospital. Do you want us to give this to him?"

Nicholas interrupted. "To paraphrase the reverend, the universe works in mysterious ways. I say finders keepers. Keep it."

The girl snatched the ring and clutched it to her chest. "You're dishonest." She about-faced and ran to the church.

The two physicians glared at Nicholas.

"What?" Nicholas asked. "I don't like kids. I don't like Reverend Samuel. And by the way, I don't need people to care. I'm a master at handling my own problems."

Aaron shrugged his shoulders. "Problems like being pregnant?"

Nicholas opened his mouth as if ready to speak, but nothing came of it.

Juliana stepped closer to him. "I think you need us."

Aaron uttered the tsk-tsk sound his grandmother used to emit whenever he misbehaved. "Life is going to get rough for you, buddy. Super fast."

Nicholas turned his back on the physicians and tramped toward his car.

14. BIRTHDAY BUN

Juliana and Aaron sat in the hospital cafeteria stirring cream into coffee and pinching off bits of a cake-size cinnamon bun the medical students presented to Aaron to celebrate his thirty-second birthday.

"Nice they jammed a dynamite-size candle in it for you," Juliana said, licking creamy icing off her fingers.

Aaron noticed the students spying to see if he and Juliana were eating the bun. "They're a good bunch."

A sixtyish-year-old surgeon in blue scrubs approached. "I'm Cecil Wilcox. Surgical oncology."

Juliana rose as if a high-ranking officer had approached. "I know who you are. I scrubbed with you when I was a med student."

Aaron gestured for the surgeon to take a seat, but yanked back his hand when Cecil rotated the chair beside Juliana and straddled it like a horse.

"Christian Beckett referred me to talk to you, Dr. Epione. Concerning one—" Cecil glanced at his note— "one Nicholas Charon. Your internal medicine patient, correct?"

"Correct."

Aaron detected Juliana's alarm but doubted Cecil did. The basketball-player-statured man appeared more mesmerized by the giant candle stuck in the bun.

"I'm Dr. Badalich," Aaron said. "The radiologist on this case."

"Hm," Cecil uttered, not attempting a greeting. "I understand your patient has a pelvic tumor that we need to whack out."

Aaron grimaced. "Whack out?"

"A term," Juliana said, "I heard daily on Dr. Wilcox's rounds."

Cecil set a patient information form before Juliana. "I understand from Mr. Beckett that his office is experiencing difficulty contacting your patient. Doesn't answer messages left for him at the courthouse and has an unlisted phone."

"Doesn't everyone these days?" Aaron asked. "Damn those unlisted mobile phones."

Cecil frowned at Aaron.

Aaron pinched off a large bite of his bun. "How many patients have you whacked so far this morning?"

Cecil gave Aaron the evil eye. "I have my personal radiology team. I won't require your service. Now, I prefer to talk to this young lady alone, son."

Aaron stood. "I am not your son, and address Dr. Epione as a physician. Address her as doctor or internist or woman. Not 'young lady.'"

"Okay boys," Juliana said. "I can stand up for myself as well as order surgical consults without a business guru going behind my back."

Cecil lopped off a fist-size hunk of bun and walked away.

"The nerve," Aaron said. "My surgeon dad would never behave like that. Everybody adores him."

"Probably had good parenting," Juliana said.

The dessert-sharing couple sat in silence a moment before Aaron shoved the bun aside. "He touched my birthday bun with his whacking hands."

Juliana attempted to hide her smile. "You know he may be right. However inappropriate his language and demeanor are … this strange lifeform may have to be removed."

Aaron sank into his seat with a loud sigh of surrender.

Juliana gasped and nodded toward the entrance.

Aaron turned to see Reverend Samuel marching toward them. "Oh shit. My sweet bun is attracting all of this building's disease-carrying vermin."

Samuel was already speaking with blaring volume before reaching the table. "Did you two order a surgeon to kill our man's baby?"

"Baby?" Aaron asked, quickly standing, posturing as if ready to box. "When did we start calling this thing a baby?"

Samuel stepped back far enough he could focus on Aaron's face without aid of his reading glasses. "What else do you call a pregnancy?"

"It's only ten o'clock," Juliana said, "and the men of this institution are already jockeying for first-place asshole."

She pounded the table and screamed, "Cool it, dudes."

The group of observing med students snapped photos and video of the spectacle with their cellphones, posting to Facebook and TikTok faster than Samuel could stomp out the door.

15. GOSSIP AND SAINTS

Nothing unites humans quicker than gossip. Anthropologists theorize gossip enhanced evolving Homo sapiens to unite in groups and dominate other life forms.

Hospitals and medical communities thrive on gossip. Word of a pregnant man propagated faster than wildfires racing up drought-ridden mountainsides. Empowered by social media, Nicholas's story infatuated amateur newscasters and au courant influencers extrapolating tidbits of facts into screens chocked full of "breaking news." Both broadcast and cable channels reported headlines of "Man Impregnated by Amazon Woman" and "Texas Governor Blames Liberal Left for Pregnant Man."

In Reverend Samuel Forrest's biblical circles, gossip began as "Scientists Ponder Pregnant Man" and evolved—or devolved—to "God Impregnated a Man: The Second Coming." Followers nicknamed the pregnancy: "Messiah Baby."

When word got out that there were physicians desiring to "abort Messiah Baby," churches in twelve states organized all-night vigils in protest, chanting, "Save Baby Messiah."

After zealous followers learned and targeted Judge Charon's address, Charlotte Police ordered 24-hour security details by Nicholas's apartment's door, his building's lobby, and outside street entrance.

"I'm in prison," Nicholas yelled in the phone to Juliana. "I can't even swim in my pool."

"How are the cramps doing?" Juliana asked.

"Like my insides are being sucked out."

"That's because ligaments and muscles are stretching to support the expanding uterus."

"Fuck that. Don't speak to me like I'm a pregnant

woman."

"Have you been watching the news?"

"The US house leader sponsoring a bill to declare me a protected national treasure?"

"I imagine you are feeling anxious, depressed. I would."

"There are no adjectives for how I feel. And no matter how often I piss, my bladder never stops feeling full."

"The uterus is pushing down on your bladder."

"Stop it," Nicholas yelled. "How soon can surgeons remove this abnormal growing thing?"

"It's become complicated. North Carolina legislators are blocking surgery, saying that would be an abortion."

Nicholas screamed, "I'm a man. Men can't have abortions."

"Have you felt any kicking?"

"In my pelvis?" Nicholas's stutters tripped over his other stutters. "This thing's going to kick?"

"With its legs."

Nicholas exploded with phrases that are unquotable by this author. Lascivious enough that Juliana trembled, worrying the phrases would besiege her mind for years to come. Even when she had rotated through obstetrics and women screamed profanities from labor pains, she had not heard such bawdy, nauseating, savage language.

Juliana tried to course back to medical talk. "We have no idea if this fetus is growing normally, too slowly, at a super rate, or is severely deformed. We need to repeat radiological studies."

"Appear in a public hospital? Hell no. Crowds will rip my body apart whether condemning or well-wishing me."

"We can disguise you."

"As what? A sea cow? Hold on. There's a knock on my door."

Nicholas looked through the peephole and saw the usual day-shift officer. He opened the door. "What?"

The officer nodded to something over his shoulder. "There's a little girl behind me. She said she is delivering Girl Scout cookies to you."

When the officer stepped aside, Nicholas glared at a seven-or-eight-year-old girl. "What the fuck? Didn't I already run you off from our lobby?"

The officer stepped between Nicholas and the girl. "Watch your language. She's just a child."

Nicholas peered around the officer. "Wait a minute. You're that girl who had Reverend Forrest's ring. What the crap? How'd you find me?"

He faced the officer. "You're supposed to be protecting me, asshole."

Nicholas slammed his door.

16. IN THE LIMELIGHT

Wearing a hoodie, Nicholas descended from his apartment tower and slipped through protestors crowding the plaza in front of the museum. Passing a slant-leg canopy, he overheard protestors recruiting pedestrians. "Please sign our petition to protect Baby Messiah."

Beneath a neighboring canopy, a woman dressed in a tunic extending to her feet, sat by a wooden trough bearing straw and a plastic doll wrapped in wool. Duct-taped to the manger, a sign stated, "Protect Virgin Birth Baby Messiah."

Nicholas galloped across Tryon Street, tightening his headphone apparatus to block out a sidewalk chorus singing Handel's *Messiah*, belting out "For Unto Us a Child is Born" as boisterously as the 360-member Mormon Tabernacle Choir.

He hastened through The Green, an uptown park where a lone guitarist-singer's portable amplifier dominated the air. Even though Nicholas welcomed the tranquility of Cat Steven's "Moonshadow," he pined for the comfort of immersing himself in familiar issues: larceny, prostitution, domestic violence, and urinating in public.

He approached the court complex through the Third-Street back entrance and stumbled upon Judge Marion Sanchez pacing outside his chambers.

"I don't know if you are aware of the ruckus out front," Marion said, "and I know nothing of the factual circumstances, but are you capable to work today?"

"What ruckus?" Nicholas asked, fearing more Baby-Messiah blitzkriegs.

"Come look out a front window."

Two dozen protesters on Fourth Street were picketing

and shouting, "Charon, Charon." Half of their signs declared, "Son of Satan is Coming," and the other half, "Aliens Implant Monstrous Life Form in Male Judge."

Marion watched Nicholas's well-tanned face turn shades lighter as he staggered, almost tumbling onto the marble floor.

"You should sit." Marion guided Nicholas to a bench and gave him a moment to regain awareness of his surroundings. "We don't know one another well. You are private—an enigma to most of us—but know that I'm here for you. What's all of this about?"

Nicholas shook his head, stood in place to assure his vertigo had subsided, and walked toward court.

Marion yelled after him, "I'll be in my office if you need anything."

Nicholas's first case was a middle-age woman who over the years had spent homeless-shelter funds she had solicited to purchase personal jewelry and sailboats. "My family deserved them."

His second case was a man stalking a woman in an adjoining apartment. He had drilled a small hole into her bedroom wall to watch her undress and used luggage trackers to tail her. "I was protecting her."

Both cases pleaded not guilty, and Nicholas announced he would set trial dates.

Between cases, he spotted various attorneys and clerks gawking through a side door and pointing at him.

His third case of the morning was a woman who had an abortion in the fourteenth week of pregnancy, two weeks beyond what North Carolina law allows.

Nicholas silently reviewed her summary. Mimi Gayle had lost her job when her tile-company employer downsized due to Covid obliterating demands for construction and remodeling. She sought new employment to no avail. Being unmarried, living alone, and abandoned by her boyfriend, she decided she could not support a child financially or emotionally.

Ms. Gayle sought an abortion from a gynecologist who straddled practicing in Virginia and North Carolina, and who agreed to perform the abortion, declaring the duration of her pregnancy as indeterminate.

A clinic nurse, however, thought overwise and reported Mimi and her gynecologist. Both were charged with H felonies, a class that also includes assault by strangulation and advocates sentences up to thirty-nine months.

Nicholas read and reread the charge document before he was capable to speak the "A" word aloud. "You are accused of violating North Carolina's law on abortion. Is that your understanding?"

Mimi's lawyer spoke for her. "Ms. Gayle was on the cusp of being twelve weeks pregnant when she had the abortion. The exact date of conception was equivocal. The criminal summons issued by a non-medical magistrate was guess work. Not scientific. Not factual. Ms. Gayle is not guilty of violating the abortion law of North Carolina—a law that our own governor vetoed."

"A veto," Nicholas added, "that was overridden by the North Carolina legislature. Let me remind you, this court follows the law."

Mimi's lawyer remained stone-faced.

"Ms. Gayle?" Nicholas scanned a paragraph. "I see you and your boyfriend broke—"

Mimi's lawyer interrupted. "Fiancé, your Honor."

"Fiancé then. Broke up. How long was the breakup prior to your abortion?"

"I object, your Honor. You are asking my client to testify. She is not on the stand. Has not been sworn in. She has not—"

"Yes yes yes." Nicholas skimmed the document and

turned to the district attorney. "Mr. Rockwell? Does the state have a case worthy to go to trial?"

"Yes, your Honor. Ms. Gayle admitted she and her fiancé had not engaged sexually for five months—that is twenty-two weeks—prior to her abortion. She refuses to confirm or deny sexual activity with other men after their breakup. We believe her pregnancy exceeded the twelve-week, six-day limit specified by our legislature. We have sufficient evidence to proceed to trial."

Nicholas stared again at the document and then at ceiling lighting, long enough that both lawyers and all attendees peeked at the ceiling, attempting to discern what could be alluring.

"Your Honor?" the defense attorney asked.

He waited and then asked a second time.

Nicholas finally looked at the district attorney, at Ms. Gayle and her lawyer, and then at the backrow of the room.

Behind the backrow, a seven-or-eight-year-old boy stood alone, staring at Nicholas. The boy was as catatonic as the metal-statue children in the Wells-Fargo-Plaza fountain.

Was there a conspiracy of children out to torture him? Court is no place for children—much less on a day of arguing sex and abortions. Had parents been so enveloped in hallway gossip as to ignore a child wandering away?

"Bailiff? Escort that child from this courtroom. Find the parents. Threaten them with a stiff fine if ever again their urchin wanders about our court complex."

While waiting, Nicholas mumbled beneath his breath, "Children are vermin invading every opportune crack and cranny."

Once the bailiff returned and shrugged no luck, Nicholas pointed a knuckle at the defense lawyer. "I shall make my determination first thing Monday for a trial date." He turned to Mimi. "I am curious, Ms. Gayle. If timing does not support your claimed brevity of pregnancy, what possible explanation do you—or you and your able lawyer—have for how you became pregnant?"

"Your Honor," Mimi's lawyer yelled. "I object. This is neither the time nor place for—"

Nicholas pounded his gavel. "Quiet." Nicholas sat dazed while the phrases "immaculate conception" and "virgin birth" sped circles in his mind like a runaway carousel.

Judge Marion Sanchez appeared with a second woman judge she had summoned. Both stood in the back of the court with scolding stares and arms crossed like petulant football coaches glaring at a losing game.

Nicholas vaulted to his feet as quickly as if someone had screamed, "Fire."

The stunned bailiff sprang to attention and announced, "All rise."

Nicholas fled to his quarters, yearning to hide as if back in childhood, hiding in his closet as he had done whenever his mother disciplined him.

17. MARSHALL PARK

After Nicholas refused to surface from his office and return to court, the two judges who had observed him, divided assuming and rescheduling his remaining cases.

At midday, Nicholas emerged, slinked along hallways, snaked through the courtyard, and crossed the street to Marshall Park. Perhaps the ducks and geese by the pond would provide a respite.

But then he saw him.

The boy who had stood behind the backrow.

He was sitting on the ground with his face buried against his bent knees and crying. Not sniffling, but wailing.

Nicholas surveyed the park, but no adults were present. He felt conflicted by his options: returning to the assaults of his apartment building, the inferno of court, or the purgatory of dealing with a sobbing, lone child.

His urge was to jog—not to home—but throughout uptown, maybe to South End or farther—to the end of earth if he could escape escalating misery.

But then he felt it.

Definitely felt it.

A kick in his pelvic area.

Being informed he was pregnant had been a loathsome intellectual exercise. But a kick? That was beyond scientific discourse. That was fucking reality. Changing venues would not be an escape. Jogging would not be an escape. Standing motionless would not be an escape. Holding his breath long enough to pass out would not be an escape.

He found himself yearning to sit by the boy, bend his knees, bury his face into his knees, and join the sobbing.

But then a strange thought—strange to him—derailed

him from following his urges. What if that squatty position harmed the baby within him? It was the first time he pictured what pregnancy meant. There was new life within him.

Fuck that, he thought. That's woman tripe. I'm a man. A fucking championship swimmer. A judge. A jogger. Not a squeamish, over-protective, obsessing prissy girlie.

"What's the matter?" a small voice called out.

Nicholas peered down. The boy on the ground was staring up at him. "What?"

"You're talking to yourself. Are you a crazy park person?"

"I beg your pardon. I was thinking, not talking."

"You were talking."

"Okay then. What did I say?"

"You said, 'prissy girlie.'"

"Shit." Nichols circled the boy while covering his face with his hands. "Pardon the language. I am having a bad day."

"Are you going to hurt me?"

Nicholas uncovered his eyes. "Why would I hurt you?"

"My father went crazy and gave me a black eye. Twice."

"No, no. I'm not crazy—not psychiatry-like crazy. Crazy about what's happening. You can count on that. But you are safe. Everyone around me is safe. Only I am not safe. Go back to what you were doing."

"I was crying."

The next phrase out of Nicholas's mouth should have been, "Why?" And he knew that. But then he would be ensnared. Forced to listen to a child's story. Probably a tragic, complicated, rambling story. He had no time for that. So, he said, "Maybe your day will get better."

The boy stared hard at him. "It won't."

Another trap. Maybe this kid has a routine. Is a grifter. Maybe he should walk away.

The boy again buried his face. If he resumed crying, would it be for real? Or part of a routine?

Nicholas quickly asked, "Where are your parents?"

The boy picked at his shoe laces. "My mother died when I was born. My father is locked up somewhere. My uncle took me in—my father's brother."

"Where is your uncle?"

"We were moving from Atlanta to somewhere in New Jersey. He stopped at the Sheriff's office and left me in the waiting room. I waited and then searched. He wasn't there. Nobody remembered him. I ran to the parking lot. His car was gone."

"Maybe you checked the wrong parking lot."

"That was two days ago."

Nicholas's jaw dropped. "Where did you sleep the past two nights?"

"By the duck pond."

Nicholas yelled, "In the park at night?"

The boy remained motionless.

Nicholas knelt beside him. "Why would your uncle abandon you?"

"He lost his job. Can't afford me."

Nicholas felt he was back in court, but without a wrong-doing adult to punish. "Do you know his mobile phone number?"

"He couldn't pay his bill. They cut his service."

Airtight helplessness. This was the very reason he didn't date, didn't have children, didn't desire relatives, didn't obtain a pet. "Do you have identification?"

"Like what?"

Airtight.

"Do you have a social worker?"

The boy shook his head.

"Someone should call social services for you. Those people are paid to handle situations like this."

The boy reached into a small sack and threw seeds toward the ducks with the force of wanting to burn a catcher's hand with a hard pitch.

The ducks ignored the pitched seeds.

Nicholas mumbled, "Ducks don't eat seeds. They like green food. Grasses. Where did you get that sack of seeds?"

The boy pointed toward the base of an oak. "Someone left it over there."

Nicholas mumbled, "Of course, they did."

After watching a duck make a crash-landing on the pond, Nicholas extended his hand to the boy. "Come on. I'll walk you to the Sheriff's office. They'll know what to do."

"I already asked them. They said it wasn't in their job description."

"They what?"

The boy shrugged. "What they said."

"That's completely wrong. They should have driven you to social services—child services."

"Can you drive me there?"

"My car is over a mile away." Nicholas paced a moment, weighing options. "I can't drive a stray kid in my car. I could be accused of kidnapping."

The boy pouted a moment. "I might as well."

"You might as well what?"

"Get kidnapped."

This kid is really good, Nicholas thought. We'd walk to my apartment, he would want to go to the bathroom, he would see how nice my place was, he would refuse to leave. Make up lies about me if anyone asked why I had him there. Airtight.

Again, he felt a kick in his pelvis and grabbed his belly. "Fuck."

The kid frowned. "What's wrong?"

"Indigestion. It's a long story—a nightmare."

Nicholas recognized the boy's yearning stare. It was the stare of wanting something like a pup eager for its master to toss a ball. "Wait here. I'll get someone from my staff to help you."

"Sure you will," the boy muttered, and again buried his face in his knees.

Nicholas crossed Third Street and got as far as the court-complex plaza before stopping.

What the hell am I doing, he thought. All of Charlotte is out for my blood. I can't pile on another agony.

He pulled his hoodie over his head and headed toward home, thinking, I'm glad I didn't ask the boy his name. I would have felt responsible.

18. SHE'S EVERYWHERE

As Nicholas stepped from his building's elevator onto the thirty-seventh floor, he happened upon movers rolling stacked cardboard boxes toward the end of the hall.

A woman was examining the boxes. "These go to the kitchen."

She noticed Nicholas stopping at a door and pulling out his keys. "Hi. I'm Violet Triplett. Your new neighbor. My son and I are moving here from Wilmington."

Nicholas nodded, unsettled that his security detail was missing. "In that case, welcome—I guess."

"Seems like a nice building."

"Uh … Pretty much."

"I'm a physician assistant. By living in this building, I can simply walk a few blocks and bingo. I'm at my clinic. How cool is that?"

"Somewhat cool."

The woman applied more lipstick to her already overly red lips. "Where do you work?"

"Uh … six, seven blocks away. Bit of a walk."

"So, similar." Violet was interrupted by her young son emerging from their apartment and charging toward her. "Mom? Did you know there's a pool on the roof? Can I go see it?"

"Not by yourself. When I finish supervising the movers, honey, I'll go with you."

The boy huffed and whined. "But that'll take all day."

Nicholas felt his stomach sink and shoulders jerk when the boy pivoted and looked at him. He was the boy from the park.

As Nicholas stared, the boy frowned at him.

Nicholas stepped back for a fuller look. "You were just in the park."

The boy spoke with a sheepish tone. "What?"

"Marshall Park. Twenty minutes ago. You were there. We talked."

The boy slid behind his mother, partially hiding as he peeked at Nicholas.

Violet squinted with confusion. "You must be mistaking him for someone else. We arrived in Charlotte two hours ago, haven't been anywhere but here."

Nicholas stared at Violet without speaking, trying to sneak better views of the boy.

Violet clutched her son's shoulders and shoved him toward their apartment. "Honey. Go inside. Show the movers which boxes go to your room. Wait there until I say you can leave."

Nicholas looked down at the boy's hands. He was holding a small sack identical to the seed sack in the park.

The boy disappeared into their apartment as Violet approached another mover stepping off the elevator. While directing the mover and following him, she ignored Nicholas as if he were invisible.

Once inside his apartment Nicholas locked his bolt lock and checked it three times.

Children often look similar, he thought, but he had no doubt this was the same boy who had been in the park.

He could feel his heart pulsating in his neck and sweat oozing form his face and armpits, enough that he chilled and trembled.

He rarely drank alone, but poured himself a glass of bourbon, took a sip, and then slugged down the remainder.

He also rarely stepped onto his thirty-seventh-floor balcony, but felt the urge for fresh air and a view of his city. But Charlotte felt unfamiliar. Unfamiliar in the manner his own body had grown to feel unfamiliar.

Everything had changed and he had no control. Even

his brain had changed, erupting with unfamiliar moods. And now he was not trusting what he saw. Did the boy down the hall have the same seed sack or not? Was he the same boy? Or was Nicholas's imagination deluding him? No. What he had seen was real. But what did it mean?

Within minutes, Nicholas raced to the elevator—forgetting to bolt his door—descended to the parking garage, and sped to Marshall Park. He parked illegally on the street and jogged to the duck pond.

By the pond, the boy was crouched and crying.

Nicholas knelt beside him and whispered, "I brought my car. I'll drive you to social services."

The boy looked up. His face was dirty enough that currents of tears had worn through grime to create streaks of clear skin. "For real?"

"For real."

Nicholas extended his hand and helped the boy to his feet. "Do you need something to eat or drink?"

The boy had a vacant look like people craving for something they can never have. "It's been two days."

"What do you want? A hotdog? Cheeseburger? French fries?"

"Anything," the boy mumbled.

"What's your name?"

"Eric. What's yours?"

"Nicholas. There's a People's Market on our way with all kinds of food."

Nicholas pulled out a handkerchief, dipped it in the pond, and wiped the boy's face.

The boy's lips quivered. "Thank you."

Nicholas electronically lowered the soft top on his convertible sportscar, wowing Eric who stretched his neck to take in the sights as they drove through a mixture of high-rise and two-story buildings.

Nicholas could not explain it, but the food at the

market tasted far better than he remembered it tasting. He enjoyed watching Eric inhale food, and beyond that, he was enjoying being immersed among parents busy with children, feeding them, disciplining them, wiping their noses, cleaning spills, laughing.

At Child, Family, and Adult Services, Nicholas felt loss as the social worker accompanied Eric to another room. Enough barrenness that he remained sitting in the lobby long after Eric was gone, watching employees interact with children. A new feeling emerged, a sensation reminiscent of taking a hot bath, or lying on summer grass studying the Milky Way, or smelling breakfast cooking to pull him out of bed.

As he walked out of the building, he heard Eric yell his name. He turned and watched the boy run toward him, out of breath and panting. "I was afraid you left before I could thank you."

"You are most welcome. I hope life gets better for you. You deserve that." Nicholas reached into his pocket. "Give my card to your worker—in case you need anything. Or you call me."

Eric studied the card but said nothing.

"Take care of yourself," Nicholas said, and ruffled Eric's hair.

"I will. You too."

Eric reached out with one hand and pressed his palm on Nicholas's abdomen, backed away, and looked up at him. "You are a good person."

Nicholas watched Eric run back into the building.

He was dumbfounded. What had Eric meant by touching him in the same manner of the old woman?

But soon, Nicholas was smiling, whistling as he strolled to his car.

The sun seemed brighter and the air fresher as he drove toward uptown, whistling an unnamed but cheerful tune he retrieved from boyhood, a tune his mother used to hum before and after reading him bedtime stories.

As he slowed for traffic, moving his foot to the brake, he realized his belly felt different. More flexible. Lighter.

He rubbed his abdomen. The muscles felt more relaxed.

As if on autopilot, he abruptly braked, pulled to the curb, leapt from his car, and rubbed his abdomen.

The lump was gone.

What the hell?

He kept palpating as if he had lost something he was driven to find. But the lump—whatever it had been—was not there.

He parked at the Baptist Church and sat beneath the tree where the old lady had tossed seeds.

Previously, there had been bald spots in the lawn, but now the carpet of green was complete.

He doubted the woman would return—at least not as an old lady—but knew that someway, she was all around him—in people surrounding him—people needing him—people he could help—people who could show him the way.

He sat on the grass, bent his legs so he could rest his face upon his knees, and wept.

Life felt good.

DC Fidler (Author)

A native of the North Carolina Appalachian Mountains, DC Fidler lives in Charlotte, North Carolina.

He has combined a career in academic psychiatry and cultural psychiatry with a lifetime of playwriting, acting, directing, composing music, and teaching creative writing and the dramatic arts.

He is an award-winning playwright, author of the textbook: *Psychiatry for Actors: Building a Character Using Psychiatric Principles*, author of short stories, author of novels: *Boogieban*, *Wood Whisperers*, *Dangerous Art*, and co-author with RJ Casey of the novel: *Green Lights of Baghdad*.

Plays, Novels, and Textbooks by DC Fidler

Novels and Textbooks
- Boogieban
- Wood Whisperers
- Dangerous Art
- Green Lights of Baghdad (With RJ Casey)
- Psychiatry for Actors: Building a Character Using Psychiatric Principles

Plays
- Voices in the Woods
- Guilt by Association (With RJ Casey)
- Three Diaries
- Sir William Bowlinggreen and Company
- Shiraz
- Anniversary of Miss Nanette Pringle
- School Children Hiding Under Desks
- Grams
- Camp Uni
- Boogieban (Two-Actor Version)
- Boogieban (Seven-Actor Version)
- Ahulaqs
- Elk and Wolf (With Travis Teffner)
- Santee Delta (With Travis Teffner)
- Celtic Crossing
- Stone Touchin'
- Daugherty Park Merry-Go-Round
- La Dynastie
- The Last Farm
- Gyges
- Begat
- Hijacked Lives

- Five X

Short Plays
- Persons
- Cruise
- Mobile to Where
- Oman Truce
- Second Amendment
- The Greek God Club
- Microscopic Misconceptions
- Drone Guns
- Moon Bugs (With Travis Teffner)

Screenplays
- Green Lights of Baghdad (with RJ Casey)

Short Stories and Novelettes
- Recipient
- The Dust Portal
- Charon: A Modern Myth

Musicals
- Pied Piper (With Lauren Horacek)
- Healer Man
- Medicine Show